key to reading™

At Key Porter Kids, we understand how important reading is to a young child's development. That's why we created the Key to Reading program, a structured approach to reading for the beginner. While the books in this series are educational, they are also engaging and fun – key elements in gaining and retaining a child's interest. Plus, with each level in the program designed for different reading abilities, children can advance at their own pace and become successful, confident readers in the process.

Level 1: The Beginner

For children familiar with the alphabet and ready to begin reading.

- Very large type
- Simple words
- Short sentences
- Repetition of key words
- Picture cues
- Colour associations
- Directional reading
- Picture match-up cards

Level 2: The Emerging Reader

For children able to recognize familiar words on sight and sound out new words with help.

- Large type
- Easy words
- Longer sentences
- Repetition of key words and phrases
- Picture cues
- Context cues
- Directional reading
- Picture and word match-up cards

Level 3: The Independent Reader

For increasingly confident readers who can sound out new words on their own.

- Large type
- Expanded vocabulary
- Longer sentences and paragraphs
- Repetition of longer words and phrases
- Picture cues
- Context cues
- More complex storylines
- Flash cards

Ruby and Louise
were making a sign.

Max and Morris
were playing.

Max loved his yellow truck.
So did Morris.

"Mine," said Morris.
Morris would not share.

Max loved his white ambulance.
So did Morris.

"Mine," said Morris.
Morris would not share.

Max loved his red train.
So did Morris.

"Mine," said Morris.
Morris would not share.

Louise loved the new sign.

So did Ruby.

Max loved his
Jelly Ball Spitting Spider.
So did Morris.

"Mine," said Morris.
A blue jelly ball flew out.

It hit the sign with a…

splash!

**Morris gave Max the
Jelly Ball Spitting Spider.**

A yellow jelly ball flew out.
It hit the sign with a splash!

Bunny Scout Leader
loved the new sign.

**"Whose idea was it to add
the splashes of colour?"**

"Mine," said Max
and Morris together.

CUT ALONG DOTTED LINES